THE COOKIE MAKER OF MAVIN ROAD

CANDLEWICK PRESS

Benedict Stanley and his cat, Audrey Mae, live at 23 Mavin Road.

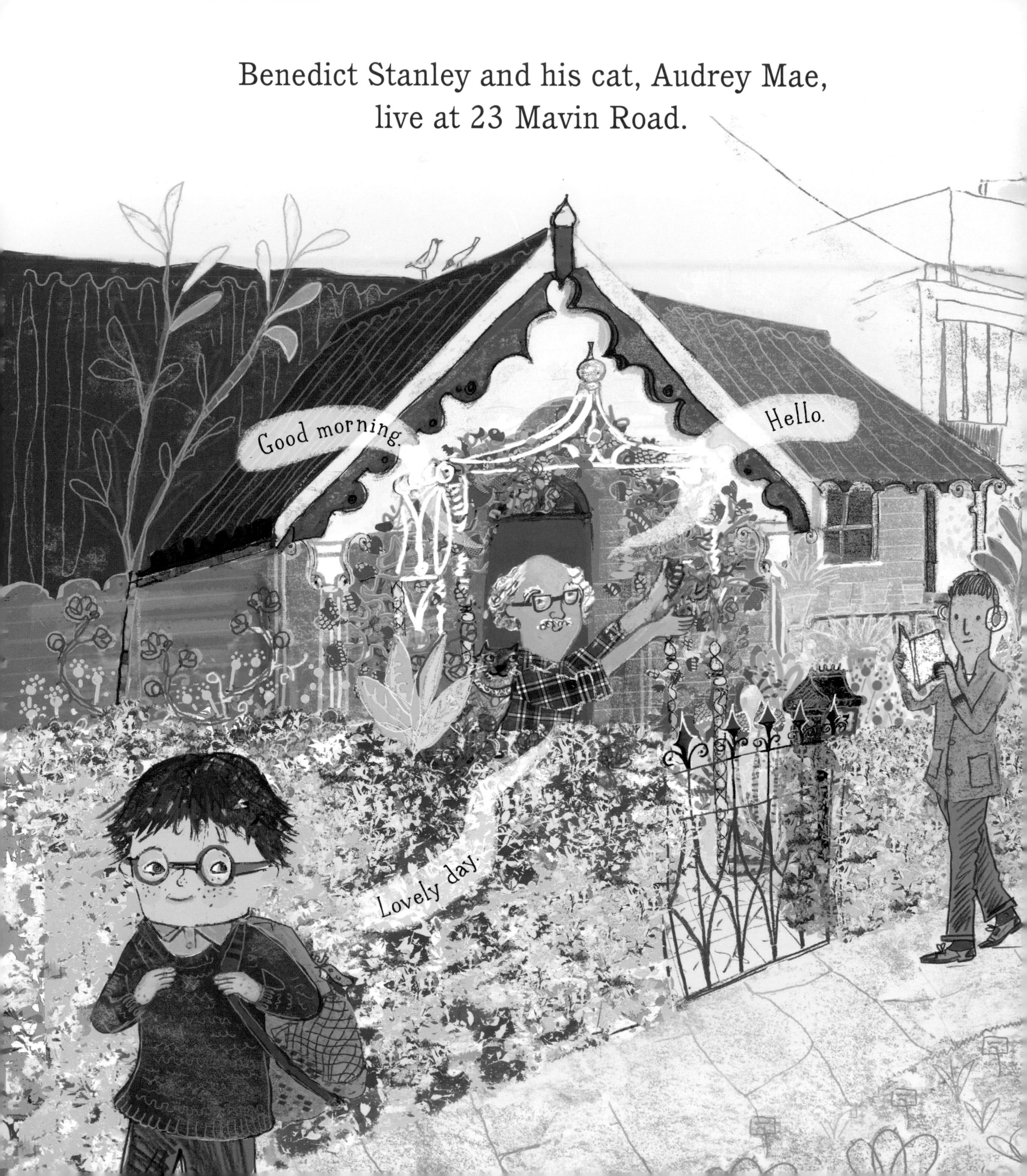

Each morning, they greet their neighbors.

But ears are too full and mouths stay closed.

"Perhaps tomorrow," Benedict Stanley sighs.

Benedict and Audrey Mae putter and plant
until legs weary and shoulders tire.
From the patio, they watch
the comings and goings
on Mavin Road.

23

"I like your cat," says a young neighbor one morning.

Benedict smiles. "Her name is Audrey Mae."

In his kitchen, Benedict Stanley
reaches for his wife's recipe book.
He sifts and folds,
shapes and bakes,
into the evening.

Before the joggers puff
and the walkers strut,
Benedict and Audrey Mae
make a special delivery.

Each morning after that,
Benedict and Audrey Mae
deliver cookies along Mavin Road.

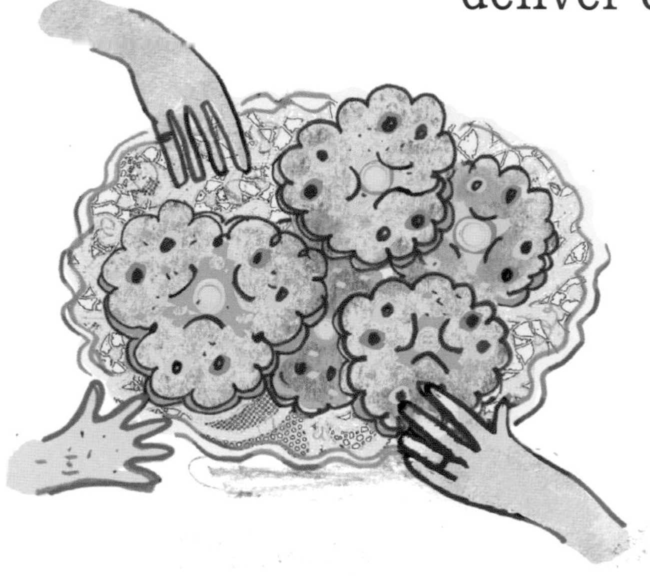

Shortbread
when triplets arrive home,

chocolate chip
to welcome new neighbors,

and ghosts and ghouls
for Halloween.

Who is making the cookies?
Someone kind.

Benedict and Audrey Mae
make cat cookies
with currant eyes
after a kitten rescue.

And soccer cookies after a tournament.

One evening, an aching and snuffling Benedict Stanley shuffles to bed.

The dance recital cookies stay on the cooling rack.

There are no bike cookies after
a ride without training wheels.

And no ambulance shortbread with cherry lights
after a tumble from a roof.

Benedict Stanley wheezes and sneezes.
Audrey Mae prowls and yowls.

Where is the cookie maker?
Perhaps she was just visiting.

Where's the cookie maker?
Maybe she's on vacation.
23

Rose petals fall
and cabbages wilt.
Outside Rory's house,
a cat prowls and yowls.

It's Audrey Mae.

Later that afternoon, Benedict Stanley
shuffles down the hall to answer
a knock at the door.

Audrey Mae
came visiting.

In the sunshine,
Benedict Stanley and Audrey Mae
watch while their neighbors
putter and prune, laugh and chat.

By New Year's Eve,
Benedict Stanley feels much better.

Audrey Mae watches
as Rory and their friends
sift and shape.

Benedict Stanley
sprinkles
and swirls
and smiles.

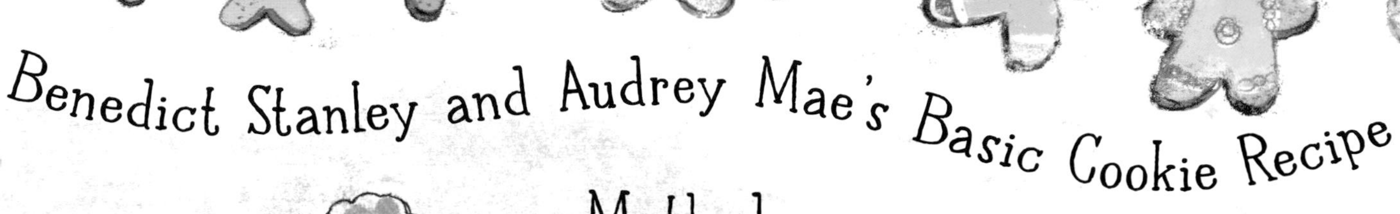

Benedict Stanley and Audrey Mae's Basic Cookie Recipe

You will need

- a bowl
- an electric mixer
- baking trays
- parchment paper
- a sifter
- a rolling pin
- a cooling rack
- icing
- an adult to help you

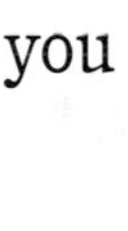

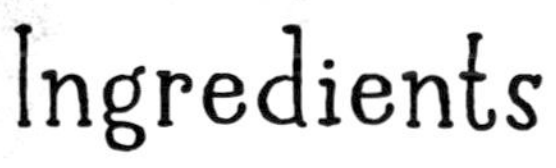

Ingredients

1 cup butter

2/3 cups sugar

1 teaspoon vanilla

1 egg

2 1/4 cups plain flour, sifted

a little extra flour for kneading the cookie dough

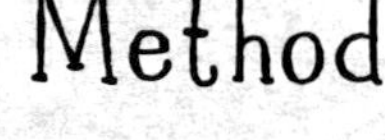

Method

Preheat the oven to 350°F (180°C).

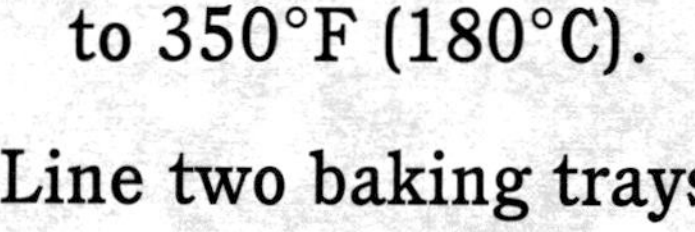

Line two baking trays with parchment paper.

Beat butter, sugar, and vanilla with electric mixer until soft and creamy.

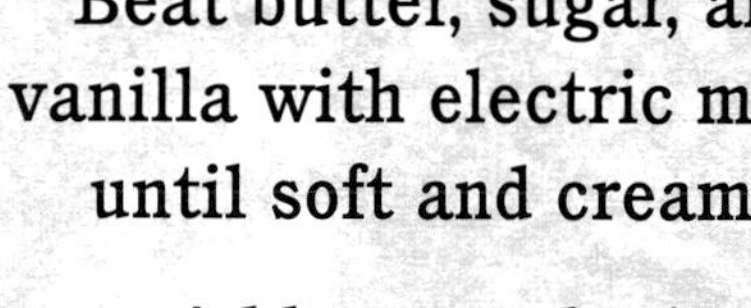

Add egg and mix until combined.

Stir in flour.

Sprinkle flour on the work area and knead the dough into a ball.

Roll the dough with a rolling pin until it's a quarter inch thick.

Cut out shapes with a cookie cutter.

Place the cookies on the prepared trays and bake for 12–15 minutes.

Cool on a rack, then ice and decorate.

To change the flavor, add chocolate chips or lemon zest.

Decorating ideas

Spread the cookies with colored icing and top them with sprinkles.

Decorate with your favorite dried fruit or candies.

Make funny faces using different candies.

At Christmas, you can turn your cookies into decorations. Make a small hole at the top of each cookie before baking. When they are cool, thread them with ribbon and hang them on the Christmas tree.

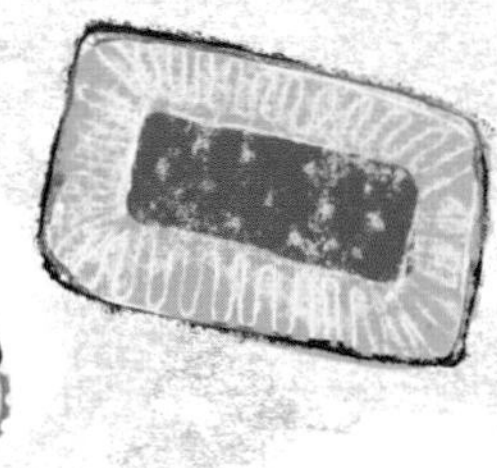

For Rugerio Rizzo—Papa.

Thank you for the stories, curiosity, and love.

SL

To my neighborly friends Rebecca, Jane, and family

LA

The author would like to acknowledge that The Cookie Maker of Mavin Road *was drafted and written on the lands of the Wadawurrung people. Wadawurrung is a clan of the Kulin Nation.*

First US edition 2021
First published by Walker Books Australia 2020

Library of Congress Catalog Card Number pending
ISBN 978-1-5362-1997-5

21 22 23 24 25 26 TLF 10 9 8 7 6 5 4 3 2 1

Printed in Dongguan, Guangdong, China

This book was typeset in ITC Cushing and Halewyn.
The illustrations were done in mixed media.

Candlewick Press
99 Dover Street
Somerville, Massachusetts 02144

www.candlewick.com